Bob's Epic Journey

By

Stewart Williams

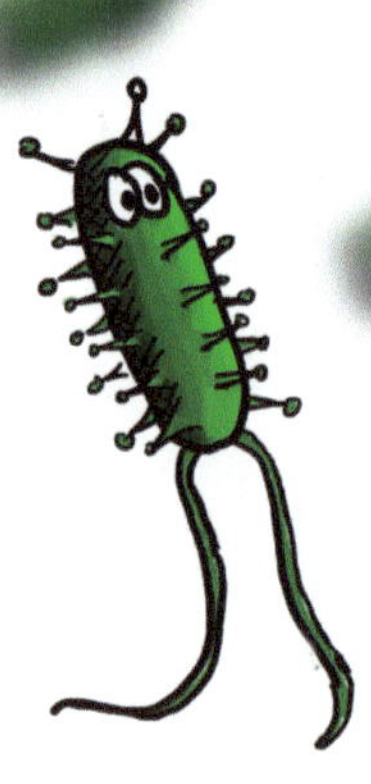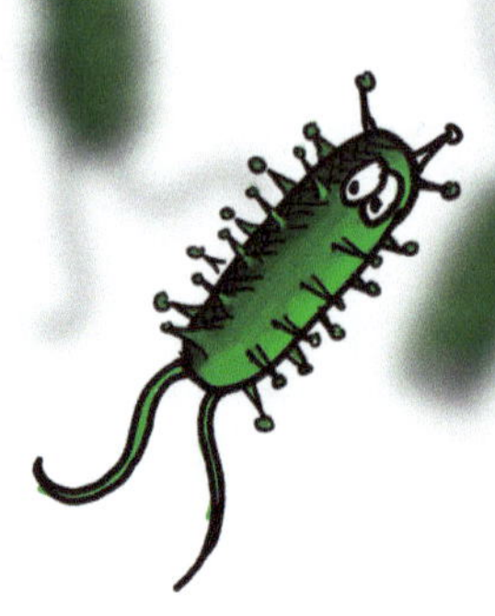

Text © 2019 by Stewart Williams

Illustrations copyright © 2019 by Stewart Williams

To Ella and Lucy.

Be like Bob! Don't let anything stop
you from achieving your dreams.

This is Bob. Bob is a bacterium.
He is small. So small, you could only see him with a powerful microscope.
Millions of years ago (even before your nan was born),
the world was full of creatures like Bob, but that was all.
Nothing else.

No birds.
No dogs.
No people.

But there was just one problem...

Bob was bored. Everyone looked the same, every day was the same.

Something had to be done.

So, after a long, long time and a lot of BIG mistakes, one of Bob's distant relatives (who as it happened was also named Bob) did something amazing...

He became a fish!

Being a fish was awesome! Not all fish look the same. So now, when he bumped into someone, he could actually tell if he had met them before.

But, there was just one problem...

It seemed that there was always a bigger fish around the corner just waiting for a chance to gobble him up.

Life in the water was simply too dangerous.

Something had to be done.

So, after a long, long time and a lot of BIG mistakes, one of Bob's distant relatives (who as it happened was also named Bob) did something amazing...

He became an amphibian!

Being an amphibian was awesome! It meant he could live in AND out of
the water. He was a lot more relaxed.

But, there was just one problem...

So, after a long, long time and a lot of BIG mistakes, one of Bob's distant relatives (who as it happened was also named Bob) did something amazing...

He grew fur and became a mammal!

Being a mammal was awesome! Now that his blood was warm, he could curl up in a cosy ball and keep himself as snug as a bug!

But there was just one problem...

Bob was constantly struck with itches he simply couldn't reach to scratch.

Something had to be done.

So, after a long, long time and a lot of BIG mistakes, one of Bob's distant relatives (who as it happened was also named Bob) did something amazing...

He became a primate! Being a primate was awesome! With his bendy new shoulders and thumbs, he could scratch any itch anywhere he wanted.
SCRATCH! SCRATCH!
But there was just one problem...

Bob wasn't very smart. He was always doing silly things and doing them the hard way. He needed brains, and lots of them.

Something had to be done.

So, after a long, long time and a lot of BIG mistakes, one of Bob's distant relatives (who as it happened was also named Bob) did something amazing...

Bob became a human! Being a human was awesome! Over the years,
Bob and his relatives did some amazing things. They learnt to...

Bob couldn't fly. He spent his days looking longingly at the sky, wishing he had wings.
Something had to be done.
So, after a long, long time and a lot of BIG mistakes, one of Bob's distant relatives (who, as it happened, was also named Bob) did something amazing...

Bob built a plane! He could finally fly! Flying was awesome!
And over the years those planes got faster...
And faster...
But there was just one problem...

The sky simply wasn't high enough. Bob desperately wanted to go into space, but planes couldn't go that high.

Something had to be done.

So, after a long, long time and a lot of BIG mistakes, one of Bob's distant relatives (who as it happened, was also named Bob) did something amazing...

Bob built a rocket! He could finally explore space.

Space

was

awesome.

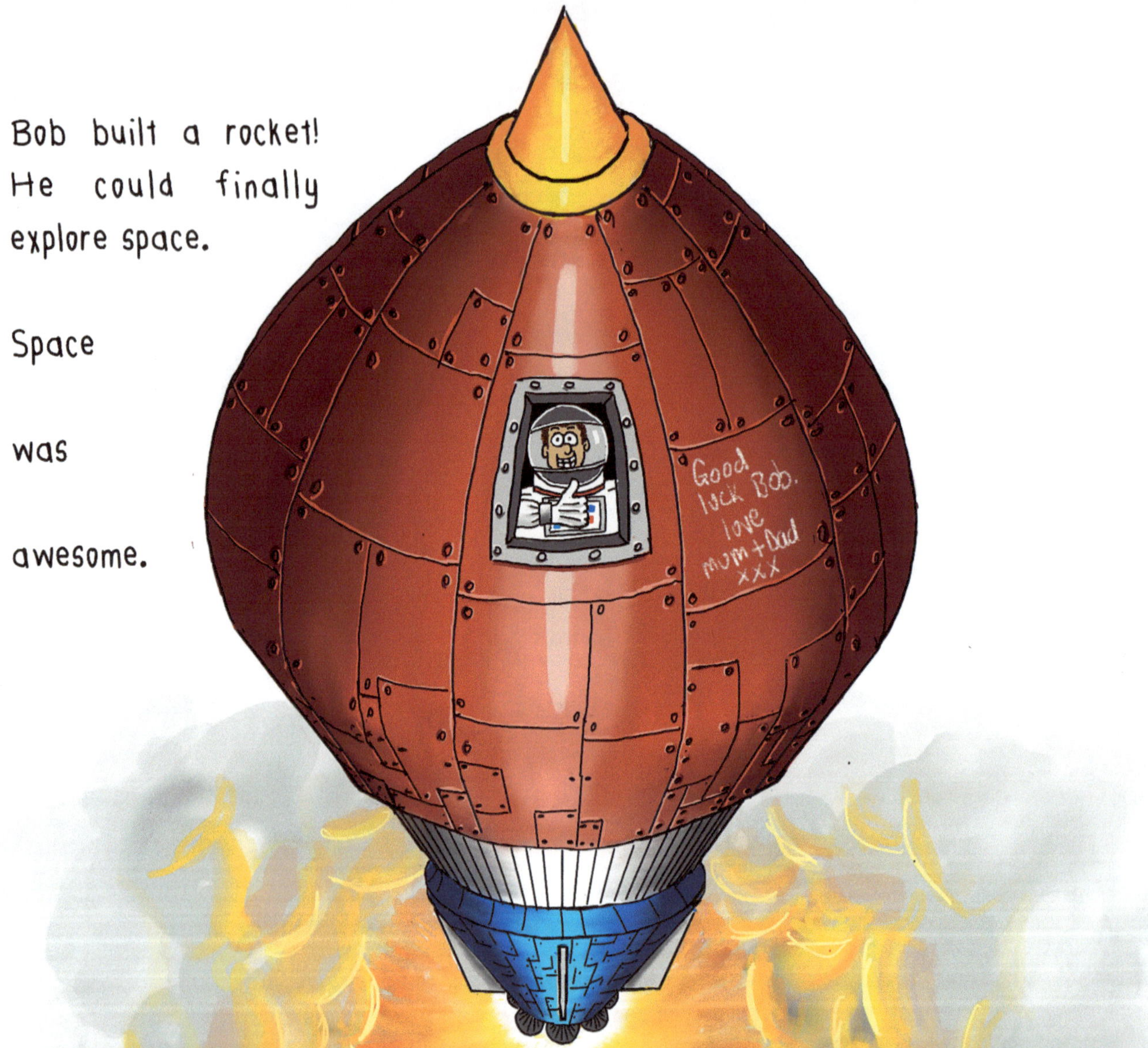

Bob could do what ever he wanted. He could float around for hours all by himself and no one was there to boss him around or to tell him to clean up his room.

But there was just one problem...

There was no room left on his space ship, and Earth was filling up quick!
FLY SPRAY
HOW TO FLY ROCKETS
Something had to be done.
So, after a long, long time and a lot of BIG mistakes, one of Bob's distant relatives (who as it happened was also named Bob) did something amazing...
ONLY PRESS THIS ONE IF YOU REALLY HAVE TO
YOU CAN PRESS THIS ONE BUT I WOULDN'T
PRESS THIS ANYTIME IT DOESN'T DO ANYTHING
PRESS THIS BUTTON!

He made a plan to start a new life on Mars. Bob built an even
bigger rocket and flew through space for a long, long time.

Finally, after months of travel, he arrived at his
new, red home. It was simply amazing.

But there was just one problem...

Bob was lonely. Although it was really cool that he was the first person to set foot on Mars, he had no one to share it with. He missed his family and friends.

Something had to be done.

Bob needed a friend.

He was determined to find life on Mars.

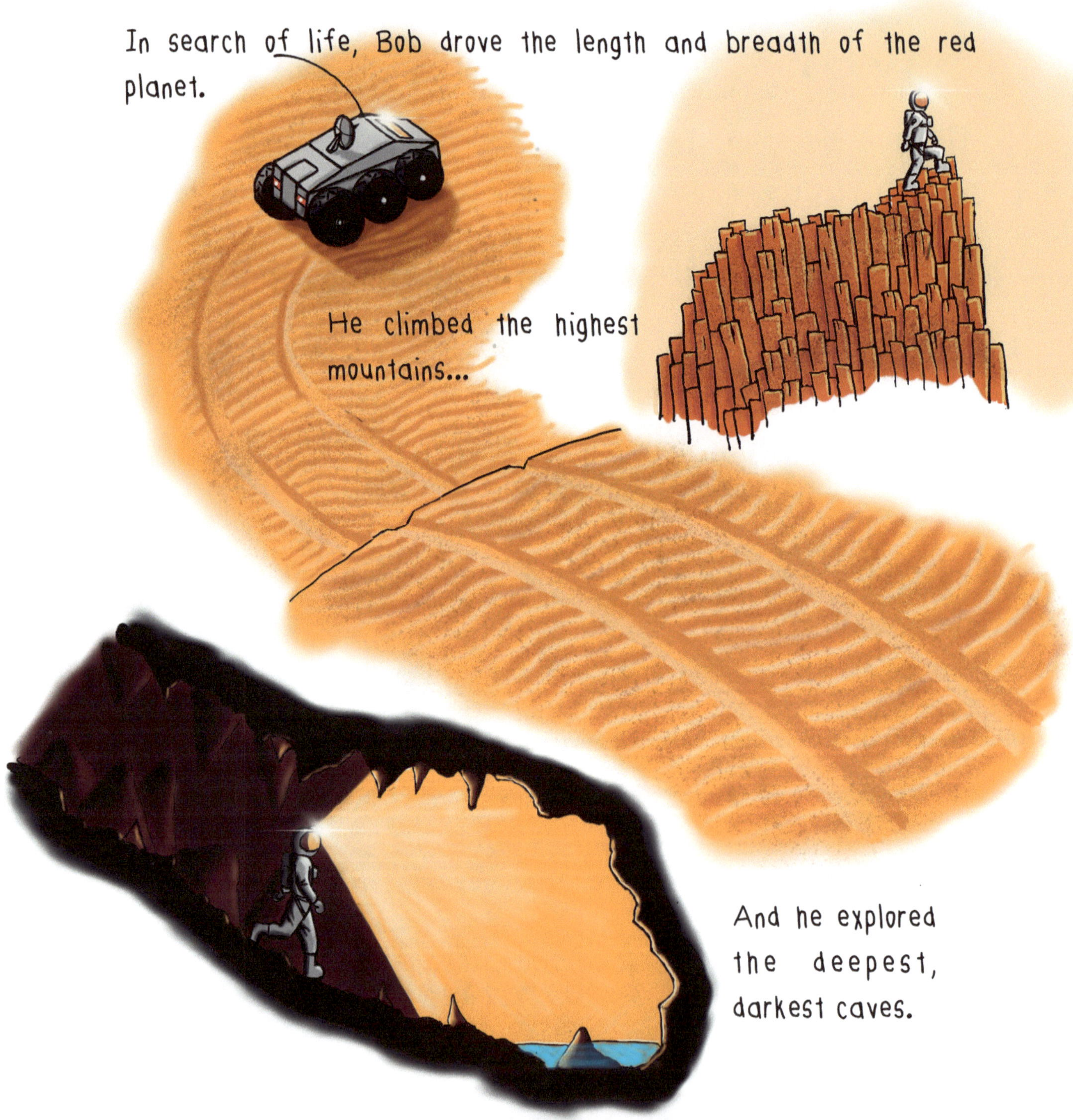

In search of life, Bob drove the length and breadth of the red planet.
He climbed the highest mountains...
And he explored the deepest, darkest caves.

And then, just as Bob was about to give up hope, at the bottom of the deepest, darkest cave, he found water. Bob knew that water was the key to life back home on Earth.

So Bob took a drop of that water back to his biodome. He looked at it through a powerful microscope and found something amazing...

A new friend...

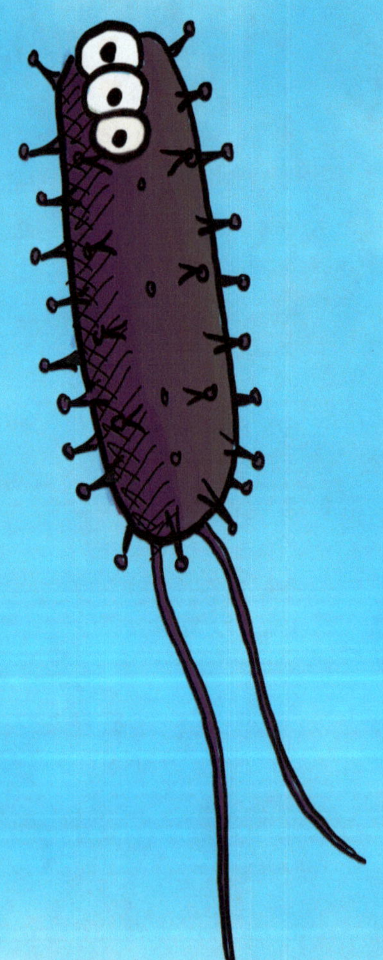

And Bob was finally happy.

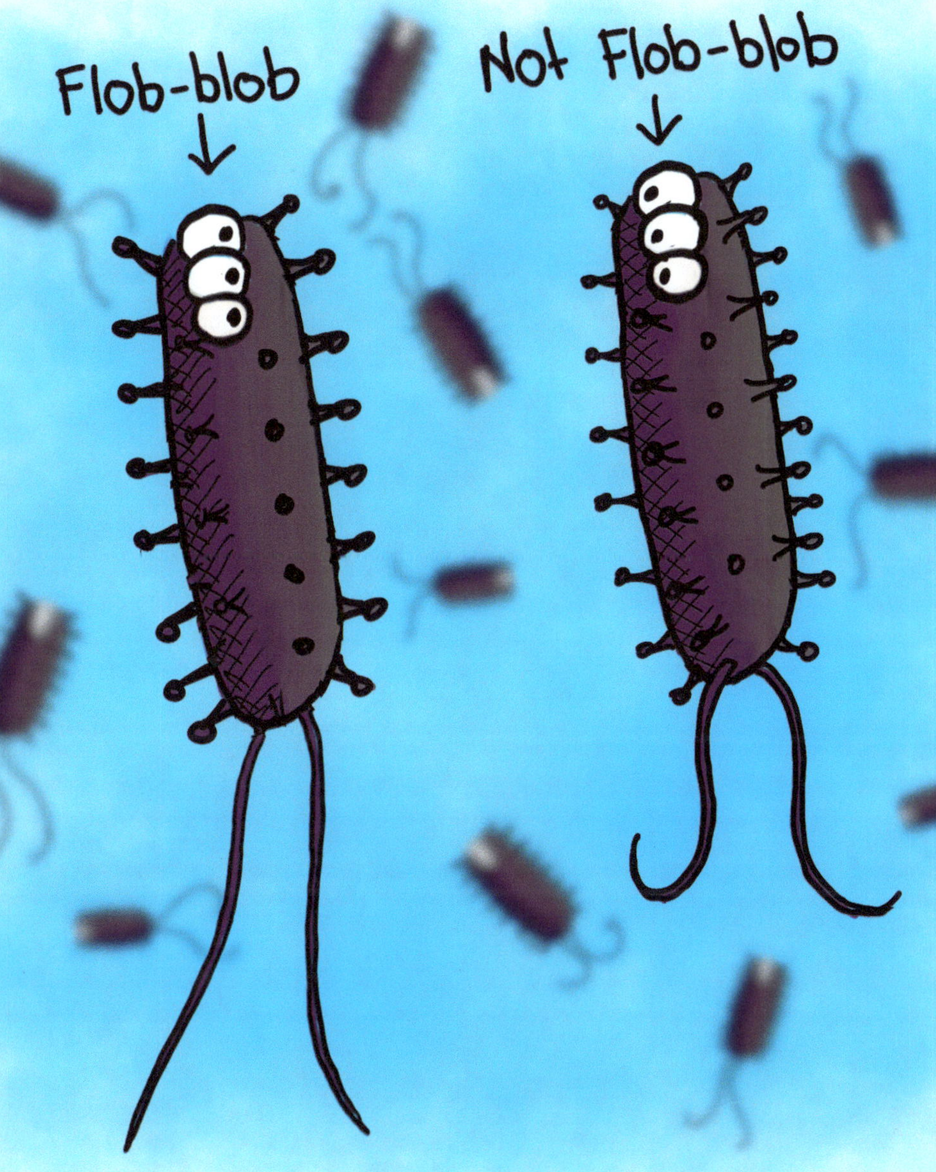

The End

Draw your own bacterium...

Hey there! If you liked this book, you might like my other books...

Available from these amazing places...
Booktopia.com.au
Email: Stewwriter@outlook.com.au
Facebook: Stewart Williams – Author/Illustrator

Or ask for them at your local bookstore.